Horsey Twinkle Toes

Peppa and George are playing in their bedroom.
"Dine-saw! Grrrrr!" says George.
Just then, the doorbell rings. Ding-dong!

It's Mr Zebra, the postman, with a parcel.
"It's probably that box of reinforced concrete I ordered,"
says Daddy Pig.

But it's not Daddy Pig's reinforced concrete.
It's a parcel for Peppa and George!
"Look at all those stamps!" says Peppa.

"A parcel! How exciting!" says Mummy Pig.
The parcel has come from Aunty Dottie, who lives in a different country, far away. She has sent a letter, too.
It says:

Dear Peppa
and George,

Here is a present
for you to share.

Love from your
Aunty Dottie

Peppa and her family open the parcel. The present has wheels, legs, a tail and a handle.

"Whatever can it be?" asks Mummy Pig.
There's one last thing in the box . . .

A horse's head – the present is a toy horse!
"I shall call it Twinkle Toes!" says Peppa.
"Horsey!" says George.
"Twinkle Toes!" says Peppa.
"Horsey!" says George.

"The present is for BOTH of you!" says Daddy Pig.
"You will have to share it. Sharing can be fun!"

Peppa and George take turns.
George is the youngest, so he gets to go first.
George likes playing with Horsey.

Next it's Peppa's turn.
"I'm Princess Peppa with my magic horse,
Twinkle Toes!"
Peppa likes playing with Twinkle Toes.

CRASH!

Peppa knocks over some
boxes in the hallway.
"I think you should play
outside where there's more
space," says Mummy Pig.

Daddy Pig thinks it's a
bit steep for Peppa and
George to play near
the house.
"I'll just ride it down
to the bottom of the
hill!" he says.
"Be careful, Daddy,"
shouts Peppa.

Daddy Pig goes too fast and lands in the duck pond!
"Silly Daddy," says Peppa.
"Did you know you have a duck on your head?"
asks Mummy Pig.

Snort!
Snort!

Hee!
Hee!

Peppa pushes George round and round the duck pond.
"Horsey!" says George.
"Twinkle Toes!" says Peppa.
It is lots of fun.

"I know," says Peppa. "Because the present's for both of us, let's call it . . . Horsey Twinkle Toes!"
"What a good idea!" say Mummy and Daddy Pig.